John A. John Alfred Poor

Memoir of Hon. Reuel Williams

John A. John Alfred Poor

Memoir of Hon. Reuel Williams

ISBN/EAN: 9783337093877

Printed in Europe, USA, Canada, Australia, Japan

Cover: Foto ©Raphael Reischuk / pixelio.de

More available books at **www.hansebooks.com**

MEMOIR

OF

HON. REUEL WILLIAMS,

PREPARED FOR THE

MAINE HISTORICAL SOCIETY.

BY

JOHN A. POOR.

READ AT A SPECIAL MEETING OF THE SOCIETY IN AUGUSTA, FEBRUARY, 1863.

PRIVATELY PRINTED.
1864.

MAINE HISTORICAL SOCIETY.

Extract from the Records at the Annual Meeting of the Maine Historical Society, held at the Rooms of the Society, in Bowdoin College, Brunswick, August 7, 1862.

"The following preamble and resolution were offered, and unanimously adopted : —

"*Whereas,* It has pleased God to call from this world the HON. REUEL WILLIAMS, one of the original members of the Maine Historical Society, we, the members thereof, place upon the records of the Society our testimony to his eminent ability, his elevated character, his social virtues, and his distinguished public services; and our respect for his memory.

"*Resolved,* That the Standing Committee be advised to invite some one familiar with his character, and of ability as a writer, to prepare an eulogium upon his character, and a memoir of his life and public services, to be publicly read at the next meeting of the Society in Augusta."

A true copy from the records.

    Attest,   EDWARD BALLARD,

                                              Secretary.

At a meeting of the Standing Committee of the Maine Historical Society, held on November 7, 1862, the following action was had : —

"JOHN A. POOR, ESQ., was appointed to deliver the eulogy on the late HON. REUEL WILLIAMS, of Augusta, in accordance with the vote of the Society."

A true extract from the minutes.   EDWARD BALLARD,

                                          Sec'y Standing Com.

MEMOIR.

Plutarch, in his Life of Solon, relates that after that great law-giver had completed his labors and established a code of laws for Athens, he resigned all his trusts, and for ten years employed himself in foreign travel, in order the more impartially to observe the workings of the laws he had framed, in the hands of others, entirely uninfluenced by any participation of his own in the administration of the government. In these travels he visited Crœsus, the renowned king of Lydia, whose fabled wealth has made his name familiar to modern times, who received Solon with all the respect due to one so distinguished for wisdom and virtue, showed him the extent of his riches and the countless means of enjoyment thereby furnished, and then asked him who he thought was the most fortunate man he had ever known. "One Tellus, a fellow-citizen of mine," promptly replied Solon, "who had been an honest man, had had good children, a competent estate, and died bravely in battle for his country." Piqued at the gravity of Solon's manner, as also by his pungent sarcasm, Crœsus in another form renewed the inquiry, gravely intimating that a man's power of present enjoyment was certainly a proof of the favor of the gods. "The numerous misfortunes that attend all conditions," said Solon, " forbid us to grow insolent upon present enjoyments, or to admire any man's happiness that may yet, in the course of time, suffer change. He only to whom Divinity has continued happiness unto the end, we call happy."

Philosophers and moralists have, in every age, speculated on the problem of human felicity, and in almost every form of language, put forth diverse theories as to the true measure of happiness or good fortune among men. But it is difficult to find, in sacred or profane writings, a more full and satisfactory definition of good fortune, of what constitutes the greatest good in life, or the true end and aim of earthly existence, than that given to us by the great Athenian teacher and law-giver. For to be truly an honest man, requires the exercise of the highest intellectual and moral qualities ; to have good children, has in every age been held to be the fruition of earthly good ; to acquire or possess a competent estate, places a man above the necessity of those practices that tend to diminish self-respect ; and to die in the public service has always been the great end of earthly ambition. To die in battle, awakens that quick sympathy of the multitude which assuages the grief of friends, and inspires courage in one summoned to the other world from this field of duty. To be wise to the last, to fulfil every private duty, and be allowed to labor to the end of life for the public welfare, which Solon regarded as the truest good, is the rarest of earthly opportunities. To be a public benefactor, and to escape the common infirmities of humanity till the measure of life is filled to fourscore, without any diminution of zeal in the public welfare, is as satisfactory proof of virtue, as, in the flush of youth and health, to fall bravely in battle.

At the departure from earth of one eminent in any of the walks of life, the upright among those who knew him instinctively review his life and history, in the exercise of unprejudiced judgment, and assign to him his proper place in the list of the illustrious dead, regardless of the popular prejudices of the hour. The accidents of fortune, the distinctions of official station, are soon forgotten, and a man's character stands forth in its true light before the world. Partisan prejudice, religious intolerance, the selfishness of unworthy minds, may for a while prevent an impartial award, but in the end every man will find his true place in the world's regard. While most fall into forgetfulness, and a few are held up as examples of warning to survivors, the true benefactors of their race are finally enrolled in the catalogue of the wise and the good.

One year ago, our Society listened with enchained attention to the Memoir of one of its original members, whose life of usefulness had led him on to that venerable age that left no companion or contemporary behind him; who seemed to glide with such quiet grace among his fellow-men of a later generation, as to seem like one from the spirit-land. That

charming Memoir of John Merrick, from the classic
pen of the Rev. Dr. Goodwin, published for this
Society, is eagerly sought for by scholars and men
of taste, as a fortunate and choice contribution to
American biographical literature.

A duty equally grateful, but far more difficult, is
imposed on one of its members to-day, in speaking
of another of its original founders, whose life, long
drawn out, was not so extended as to lose its influence or hold on the men of his own time — whose
eminent ability, elevated character, social virtues,
and distinguished public services, won for him the
respect of his associate members, and of the community in which he lived,— and who, always a leader
among men, fell, finally, at his post, in the front
rank, on the busy battle-field of life; leaving the
legacy of a wide public reputation to his country,
and the richer treasure of a good name to distinguished inheritors of his fame and fortune.

REUEL WILLIAMS, the second of twelve children of
Captain Seth Williams and Zilpha Ingraham, was
born on the second day of June, 1783, within the
limits of that part of the ancient town of Hallowell
which is now the city of Augusta. He enjoyed the
rare distinction of living, and dying, at a ripe old
age, in the place of his birth. His father, said to
have been of Welsh origin, born December 13,
1756, was a man of character and consequence
among his fellow-men; by occupation both a farmer
and a tanner. He emigrated from Stoughton, Mas-

sachusetts, in 1779, and married Zilpha Ingraham, born April 16, 1761, the daughter of Benaiah and Abigail Ingraham, who were among the early settlers of Augusta. Captain Seth Williams died March 18, 1817, at the age of sixty-one years, enjoying to the end of his life the respect of his fellow-townsmen, having filled many offices of public trust. His independent spirit and upright conduct imparted their influence to his children and others around him.

But, like most men of strikingly marked qualities, Reuel Williams derived the peculiarities of his mind and character mainly from his mother. Self-reliant, shrewd, firm, energetic, and conscientious, she had unbounded affection and every motherly virtue; and was, to the end of her life, an example of every Christian grace. She died at Augusta, September 20, 1845, in the eighty-fourth year of her age. One capable of appreciating her high qualities of mind and heart, with abundant means of judging, described her, many years ago, as illustrating every Christian virtue and every social excellence that can dignify and adorn the family circle. She merited and received the affection and respect of all who knew her, and her example and teachings bore fruit in the lives of her children.

Reuel had only the meagre advantages then afforded by the common schools of his native town till the age of twelve, when he commenced his attendance upon Hallowell Academy, boarding at home in Augusta, and walking two miles, daily, each way, to and from the school. Here he acquired a classical education, equal to the fitting of one for college, before he was fifteen years of age. On returning from the Academy in the evening, he usually went into his father's shop, and worked at the shoemaker's bench, — for his father carried on the business of a tanner and a shoemaker, — and Reuel often finished a shoe before retiring for the night. Yet he was so prompt in his attendance at the Academy every morning that Judge Robbins, of Hallowell, used to say, " I must send my sons to Augusta to board, so that they may get seasonably to school." For a short time after he reached the age of fifteen, Reuel took the place of toll-gatherer for the Augusta Bridge, which was completed in 1798, and in this way aided his father in the support of his large family, while his leisure time was carefully husbanded in study. At this period he gained the attention and acquaintance of Judge James Bridge, a gentleman distinguished for many noble qualities of character, and at that time a most prominent lawyer of the Kennebec Bar. By invitation of Mr. Bridge, young Williams entered his office as a student at law, June 25, 1798, when only fifteen years old.

Faithful and industrious, he earned his support, while a student, by writing, and accumulated in this way more than one thousand dollars before he was nineteen years of age. Judge Bridge then gave him an interest in the profits of his law business, though he was too young to be admitted to the

Bar. He invested his student-life earnings in real estate, on the east side of the river, just above the bridge, most of which, with improvements on it, he owned at the time of his death.

From the age of nineteen to twenty-one, he busily pursued his professional labors with Judge Bridge, and on reaching his majority, in 1804, was admitted to the Bar, — an event to which he had looked forward with all the pride and hope of youthful ambition.

At this time two fellow-students invited him to join them in their proposed expedition to Cincinnati, for the practice of the law. The rising fame of this new city had already begun to attract the attention of the enterprising young men of the Eastern States. Mr. Williams held this matter carefully under advisement, but finally declined the proposal, and deliberately set himself down for life in the town of his birth; — a decision that forms a striking exception in the history of the public men of this country.[1]

[1] In his latter days Mr. Williams was fond of making inquiries as to the history of Cincinnati, and as to the particular causes of the extraordinary growth of the Queen City of the West. He was of the same age as Nicholas Longworth, now the wealthiest citizen of the great West, who, a lawyer by profession, has shown an enlightened judgment worthy of his great success, and to whom, more than any one else, Cincinnati owes that success in the strawberry and grape culture, which are among the attractions of that great city, now so renowned for the wealth, refinement, and public spirit of its citizens. Had Mr. Williams established himself at Cincinnati at the age of twenty-one, and experienced the same good fortune which attended him at home, his wealth would have been equal to that of Astor.

NOTE. — *Mr. Longworth died February* 10, 1863, *since the above was*

It was fortunate for the city of Augusta, that Mr. Williams determined to remain; for to him, mainly, is the city indebted for its political and commercial importance. In his early days, Hallowell was the chief town of the Kennebec; but aided by his exertions, Augusta, without any peculiar natural advantage, became the exclusive seat of justice of the county, and finally the State Capital, where the legislative sessions have been held since 1832. In the train of these events, came the location of the Kennebec Arsenal, on which the United States Government have expended, to June 30, 1860, $265,846.91; the establishment of the Insane Hospital; and the vast influence and power which its central position, and this centralization of talent and capital, have given to Augusta; — a city of less population and wealth than some others in the State, yet superior, in the ability of its press, and the sagacious foresight of its public men, — in many respects the leading place in the State, and second in all these particulars to no capital city of the country, of similar relations.

From the time of Mr. Williams's admission to the Bar in 1804, he became identified with Augusta, and his life forms a part of its history. No work of public importance, and no enterprise affecting the Kennebec Valley, was carried forward without his direct participation in it, from that time till his death, extending over a period of nearly sixty years.

written, with a fortune estimated, by himself in 1859, at twelve millions of dollars.

His business life comprised a period of more than sixty years, dating from the time he became partner with Judge Bridge.

Judge Bridge had for years been the agent of the Proprietors of the Kennebec Purchase, an association of gentlemen of wealth, who bought of the grantees of the Plymouth Company the tract granted January 13, 1629, to William Bradford, by the Council of New England, extending from the Cobbossee Contee to Nequamkike, (Hazard Coll. vol. i. p. 298.) It was farmed out by the Plymouth Company for many years, and quite fully peopled in 1650 and 1651, when Father Dreuilletts came to Cushnoc on his fruitless mission of peace to the New England Colonists. On the 27th of October, 1661, the Plymouth Company conveyed their interests to one Thomas Winslow, through whom the title came to the Proprietors of the Kennebec Purchase.

The agency of this company was itself a large business, in the investigation of titles to real estate, in sales to be made, and proceeds to be collected. The numerous decisions in the Massachusetts and Maine Reports show the great variety of difficult and novel law questions affecting titles to real property, growing out of this business, to which the attention of Mr. Williams was directed.

"In 1807, when but twenty-four years of age," according to the statement of one familiar with his life, "Mr. Williams was brought to the notice of prominent men in Massachusetts, while engaged with Nathan Dane, in Boston, for the Plymouth Proprie-

2

tors, before the Commissioners of Eastern Lands. His engagement occupied him six consecutive weeks; and although he was junior counsel, he was highly complimented by the Commissioners on his thorough and profound legal knowledge, and the clearness and ability with which he presented and managed his case."

On the 19th of November, 1807, Mr. Williams married Miss Sarah Lowell Cony, daughter of the late Hon. Daniel Cony, of Augusta, a man distinguished in his day for his public spirit, manly virtues, and great activity in promoting the separation of Maine from Massachusetts. Mrs. Williams still survives him. Their golden wedding was celebrated more than four years before his death, with that quiet grace and dignity that always held sway in their happy home, where children and grandchildren joined in pleasant festivities in the venerable mansion, which had so long been the abode of domestic joy and undiminished affection.

Of their nine children, one son and eight daughters, five still survive. The proprieties of this occasion forbid us from entering the domestic circle, or anticipating any future eulogium.

In 1811, we first find Mr. Williams's name in the Massachusetts Reports, as counsel in a law question, in opposition to Judge Wilde, then one of the leading lawyers of the Kennebec Bar, and subsequently, for many years a judge of the Supreme Judicial Court of Massachusetts. From 1811 onward, for nearly thirty years, until he relinquished practice, on taking his seat in the Senate of the United States, Mr. Williams's name constantly occurs in the Reports, both Massachusetts and Maine, in important law cases.

In 1812, Judge Bridge, having accumulated an abundant fortune, retired from practice, leaving Mr. Williams in full receipt of the emoluments of their large business. Up to this time, the arguing of law questions had been chiefly performed by Judge Bridge, — while the office duties and labors devolved mainly on Mr. Williams, who was compelled to throw his whole strength into the work, in order to perform the routine of daily business. His studies, therefore, necessarily ran to particular questions and pending cases rather than to elementary works, and his learning as a lawyer was more the result of a large practice, calling for the investigation of points of law bearing on his own cases, than any arranged plan of study. He was not, therefore, a man of extensive law reading, beyond the investigation and preparation for argument of cases in court. This course of study gives great sharpness and clearness of legal vision. He always argued closely and logically without the forms of logic. His power of analysis and of methodical arrangement was remarkable, and contributed greatly to his eminent success.

In addition to his large practice growing out of the agency of the Kennebec Purchase, he had the charge of the Bowdoin Lands, a very large and valuable property, which he managed with admirable skill. He also had a large miscellaneous practice in which the faithful discharge of his duties was ever conspicuous. His addresses to the jury, as well as to the court, were free from any attempt at rhetorical display, but remarkable for power of condensation, concentration, and directness of argument, and, though usually brief, were effective and convincing. He was so intensely occupied in his professional labors for many years, without time for study outside them, that he was more a man of business than a man of books. But his reputation as a lawyer became widely known, and in 1815, when but thirty-two years of age, he was honored by Harvard College with the degree of Master of Arts. In 1855, the honorary degree of Doctor of Laws was conferred on him by Bowdoin College.

In 1816, in conjunction with Judge Bridge and Thomas L. Winthrop, of Boston, Mr. Williams became the purchaser of the lands, property, and remaining interests of the Kennebec Proprietors. This proved a very profitable investment, so rapid at that time was the settlement of the country. All the papers of the Proprietors, of very great historic value, came into his possession, and since his death, in pursuance of his wishes, have been placed in the archives of the Maine Historical Society for safe keeping and use.

In 1818 Mr. Williams was one of the corporators named in the charter of "The Lincoln and Kennebec Society for the Removal of Obstructions in the Kennebec River," approved February 19, 1818, and it is in and by the Act made his duty to call its first meeting, — showing him to have been the active promoter of its objects. This matter of improving the navigation of the Kennebec was always an object of his thoughts, before and while a member of the United States Senate. Appropriations to the amount of $21,100 have been expended by the United States Government for removing obstructions in Kennebec River, at Lovejoy's Narrows; $1,500 for a monument at Stage Island; and $5,750 for monuments in the Kennebec River. The sum of $45,288.56 has been expended in the construction of Seguin Light, in which is a first-class Fresnel Lens, and $6,236 on Pond Island Light, at the mouth of the Kennebec.

The separation of Maine from Massachusetts was a question in which, as is well known, Mr. Williams took an active part, giving it his earnest and effective support. In 1822 he became a member of the Legislature of Maine, and continued so for seven successive years: a member of the House in 1822–3–4–5; and of the Senate in 1826–7–8; during which time he was the active and efficient leader in the movement to make Augusta the State Capital. He was also a member of the House in 1829 and 1832, and again in 1848. To him has always been awarded the credit of the removal of the seat of government from Portland. Of the wisdom of the measure itself it is not my province to speak. Many citizens of the State deemed the removal premature and uncalled for. But the prevalence of this feeling only enhances the credit due to his talent and industry, for

2 *

its achievement, against such odds. He regarded
the question of the location of the seat of government as one addressed to the common-sense and
judgment of the Legislature, and labored for it with
a zeal and pertinacity that finally overcame every
obstacle.

In 1822 Mr. Williams was elected one of the Trustees of Bowdoin College, which office he retained for
thirty-eight years. He was ever one of the most
faithful and devoted friends of the Institution, and a
constant attendant on the meetings of the Board till
his resignation in 1860. He always looked with regret on the effort to transform this ancient and honored Institution of learning, whose catholic spirit and
liberal principles had secured for it so much popular
favor and such valuable aid from the State, into a
sectarian school, under the exclusive control of one
religious sect.

In 1822 Mr. Williams was one of the *forty-nine*
corporate members of the Maine Historical Society,
named in the Act establishing it. He had little
time to devote to historical studies or pursuits, but
he was always a faithful and consistent member,
favoring with his influence the liberal grant of aid
from the State, and paying his annual tax in early
days, when a tax on its members was the only means
of keeping up the Society.

On the 15th of February, 1825, Mr. Williams was
appointed one of the Commissioners of Maine to
divide the Public Lands, held in common with Massachusetts, under the Act of Separation, a most ardu-

ous and delicate trust, which he discharged with his accustomed intelligence and fidelity.

On the 26th of January, 1829, an event occurred which deeply affected Mr. Williams, exerting no small influence over his subsequent life,—the death of his daughter, Susan Curtis Williams, whose rare beauty, uncommon intelligence, devoted affection, and religious turn of mind, had made her an object of unusual regard in their wide family circle. The death of this daughter struck deeply to the very fountain of feeling, and seemed to soften his very nature. At times, within the last year of his life, he seemed to enjoy the opportunity of speaking of this child, describing her as possessing a purity of nature and a religious principle higher than he had elsewhere witnessed. An intimate friend of this daughter, of the same age, between whom and herself one of those mutual attachments had sprung up, which sometimes appear romantic,—survived her many years; and for her Mr. Williams always exhibited and expressed great kindness and regard. After her death, he followed with his good will the husband who survived her. He has been heard to speak of this exhibition of friendship of these young girls, as to him one of the most charming and delightful of his memories. This was the more remarkable in him, from his naturally reserved manner. He rarely spoke of himself, had few confidants, and gave out sparingly the expression of his feelings. His talent for silence, that rarest and most valuable of all mental endowments, was seldom equalled.

On the 27th of March, 1831, Mr. Williams was appointed Commissioner of Public Buildings, and superintended the completion of the Capitol, till it was fitted for the use of the State Government and the legislative sessions. This chaste and beautiful edifice is a monument to his taste and good judgment. It is so constructed that, if the public exigencies call for more ample accommodations, the hall of the House may be appropriately given up to the State Library, and better rooms for the Senate and the House provided, by extending wings in the rear, which are said to be called for by architectural rules, to give symmetry and proportion to the whole edifice. This statement is due to Mr. Williams's reputation, and to the professional experts under whose guidance it was originally planned.

On the 10th of May, 1832, Mr. Williams was appointed Commissioner of Maine, with Hon. W. P. Preble and Hon. Nicholas Emery, in reference to the Northeastern Boundary. In the discharge of this trust, he made his first acquaintance with President Jackson. Mr. Williams was originally a Federalist, and he naturally fell into the support of John Quincy Adams in the campaign of 1825, and voted for him in 1829. But on the election of General Jackson he expressed his determination to support his administration as far as consistent with his own sense of right; and he became identified from that time with the Democratic party down to the time of the repeal of the Missouri Compromise, during the administration of Franklin Pierce, which act he regarded as the commencement of troubles, and openly and unqualifiedly condemned, though an earnest supporter of Pierce's election.

In the discharge of the duties of this embarrassing Boundary Commission, Mr. Williams found in General Jackson those qualities of sincerity and frankness, that straightforward sense of justice, that won his confidence and his heart. When asked, during his last visit to Washington, to give his impressions of General Jackson, he invited the inquirer to walk to the President's Square and look at the statue of Jackson. "That statue," said he, pointing to Mills's equestrian statue, "gives you a better idea of Jackson than any portrait or any description you can find of him." In reply to the criticisms of a friend on Jackson's public conduct, he used to say Jackson was about the only person he ever knew who acted upon his own sense of right. Admitting his rude education, and that lack of self-control which can only be acquired by men of strong will in early life, he said, "he saw that Jackson's desire was to do right." In the negotiations, the Maine Commissioners, in 1832, spoke of public opinion on the subject of this treaty. "Public opinion! What is public opinion?" said Jackson. "Right is public opinion. I am public opinion when I do right."

Jackson was deeply anxious to effect, at that time, a settlement of this boundary dispute, but he could not fail to see the absurdity of the Dutch King's decision. But, said he, "what can I do? The award is not right, but what will come of the question if we reject it?" As this matter ever after occupied a large share of Mr. Williams's thoughts, and became the subject of his principal speeches in Congress, it is needful to state the question briefly, in detail, in order to show the manner in which Mr Williams presented it to Congress, and pressed the matter to a final settlement.

The history of the Northeastern Boundary Dispute goes back to the first occupation of the Continent by Europeans. France and England claimed the whole of Maine, starting together in 1602, in plans of colonization. Both granted it, with other territory, to their respective subjects, the French King, November 8, 1603, and the British monarch, April 10, 1606. The French settled at St. Croix in 1604, and the English at Sabino, August 19, O. S. 1607, from which time the Sagadahoc became the recognized boundary, though the English established trading-houses east of it. In Cromwell's time, he granted the country east of Sagadahoc to Sir Thomas Temple, and the country was peopled by the English. The French held the country east, under the name of Acadia, and the St. George River became practically the dividing line, after Sir Thomas Temple occupied east of Sagadahoc, as stated by Cardillac in his Memoir of 1692. But in 1697, at the Peace of Ryswick, the St. Croix became the boundary between Acadia on the west, and New-England on the east.

There was no recognized dividing line for the

interior, between the French and English settlements. The French planting on the St. Lawrence, in 1608, pushed back but a short distance from the river, and the English settlements were mainly along the Atlantic shore. Between the St. Lawrence and Lake Champlain, and east of it, to the Connecticut, the forty-fifth parallel of latitude became the dividing line. The conquest of Canada, in 1759, led to new colonial governments; and, in 1763, after the Definitive Treaty of Peace, the new District of Quebec was established, and the line — designed to embrace the territory acquired — followed the natural boundary, the ridge, or rain-shed, between the St. Lawrence and the Atlantic Ocean. The whole country then belonged to England, and the most simple and natural boundary was established by her, between her ancient possession, New England, and the newly-acquired territory of New France.

In the War of the Revolution New England fell into the new Government of the United States, while New France remained to England. In defining the line of boundary, the Treaty of Peace of 1783 followed the line established in 1763. Before the necessary work of running and marking this line was finished, war broke out between England and the United States, and the value, for military purposes, of a line of communication in the St. John valley, between the Upper and Lower Provinces, was then made apparent. Thereupon, England seized upon this territory, and refused to further run or mark the line, as agreed. In the Treaty of Ghent, a provision for arbitration was unfortunately agreed to by our Government, and, after declining all other proposals, Great Britain had the Dutch King appointed umpire during the administration of John Quincy Adams. His decision was, that there was no ridge, or rain-shed, separating the waters flowing in different directions, and therefore *advised* that the bed of the St. John River be adopted for the boundary. Jackson thought best, if possible, to induce Maine to consent to this decision, by offering compensation. Subsequent results have proved the wisdom of his proposal, for no State, prior to the recent rebellion, had ever been able to accomplish anything in opposition to the power of the Federal Government.

The Maine Commissioners were made the medium of an offer by Gen. Jackson, but the rejection of this award by the Senate made their report valueless, and it remained unopened till the change of parties in Maine, in 1838, led to its publication. Mr Williams saw this *" involved question,"* as it was called, in its true and simple aspect, despite the accumulated mass of confused diplomatic correspondence on the subject for so many years. He took this simple position: " It is a question of boundary ; run and mark the line, following out the words of the Treaty." This view of the question determined his future course in the Senate, and his persistent adherence to that policy forced a final settlement of the question.

It has been the fashion of the newspapers to echo the statements of British diplomatists, that " the

Treaty of 1783 left this question of boundary involved in obscurity," and some politicians of our own and other States readily fell into this notion, from indifference or an unwillingness to investigate the question itself. Any "obscurity" in the matter is much like that which an intelligent traveller would fall into, in crossing the Alps from France into Italy, in his efforts to discover a ridge on the way where Hannibal and Napoleon made attempts to solve the problem in the face of obstacles that made their exploits so famous. And we can hardly refrain from giving utterance to an expression of self-reproach as we call to mind the timidity of our own State, in finally consenting to so monstrous a folly as the subsequent surrender of so invaluable a possession on such a pretext.

The award of the Dutch King having been rejected by the Senate, no call was then made on Maine for her assent, and no progress made in the adjustment of the question, till after Mr. Williams's election to the Senate of the United States.

On the 22d of February, 1837, Mr Williams, then in the fifty-fourth year of his age, was elected, by the Legislature of Maine, to the Senate of the United States, for the term of two years, to fill the unexpired term of Hon. Ether Shepley, appointed one of the Justices of the Supreme Judicial Court of Maine. Mr Williams's term commenced on the 4th of March, 1837. He took his seat in the Senate at the extra session, on the 4th of September, 1837. He was placed on the Committees of Naval Affairs and of Roads and Canals.

His senatorial career gives him his chief claim to a national reputation. It was distinguished for its independence of party and its devotion to the interests of the whole country, not forgetting the claims of his own State. He entered Congress at the most gloomy period of our history since the war with England in 1812.

The exhaustion of individual and national resources, by the War of 1812, brought, with peace, political quiet at home, till in 1820 the slavery agitation, growing out of the admission of Missouri into the Union, gave to the thoughtful men of that time the first intimation of our present troubles, and this feeling kept alive a spirit of alarm. The war with England had stimulated party animosity throughout the country, and, under the influence of that feeling, able, ambitious men came into Congress, unschooled in the principles of the Revolutionary period. After the Peace of 1815, a new direction was to be given to public affairs. The lack of foreign topics to engross our public men, as heretofore, naturally directed their thoughts toward the Presidency, making the gratification of personal ambition the chief object of statesmanship; and the election of 1824 disclosed a number of candidates for the Presidency, without any apparent difference of opinion upon public measures. The personal preferences of Mr. Clay for John Quincy Adams gave the country that untractable administration which sought to govern without a policy, and to dispense with the ordinary fidelity of party support. The opposition united and elected Gen. Jackson, and under his iron rule, during his eight years, changed the administrative policy of the country; and the nation seemed ready to pass from a Constitutional Republic to a Democratic Despotism, in spite of the most powerful opposition under the combined leadership of Clay, Webster, and Calhoun. The contest was fierce and violent during Jackson's administration. Clay, Webster, Calhoun, Preston, Berrien, and others contended for certain principles of constitutional government, and for restraints upon executive power; while Jackson and his supporters maintained the absolutism of the Presidential will over all subordinate officers of the Government. He removed the deposits in opposition to the opinions of the Congress, and retained his appointees against the recorded judgment of the Senate as a part of the appointing power.

The popularity of Jackson swept over the most powerful opposition ever organized under our Government, and in 1836, with Van Buren's election, there came into Congress an array of talent unequalled in any other period of our history, in which Mr. Williams was to act his part. The administration of Van Buren placed its claims to support upon the question of finance and currency, then the absorbing topic of the day, and was soon joined by Mr. Calhoun, who gave to the Independent Treasury scheme his unqualified support. The defection of Mr. Calhoun and his followers from the Opposition gave a more personal turn to the debates of the

Twenty-fifth Congress than before, and the contests between Mr. Webster and Mr. Calhoun are unequalled for brilliant declamation, logical acumen, and oratorical power, in parliamentary history. As before remarked, the traditionary policy of the country had been overturned by the reëlection of Andrew Jackson. The Secession troubles of that period were temporarily healed or abated, under the enactment of the Compromise Tariff of 1833, and the large importations of 1835 and 1836 aggravated the coming troubles — ending in the wide-spread commercial revulsion of 1837. Individual and national bankruptcy was staring every one in the face, and the new President, Van Buren, summoned an extra session of Congress, on account of the suspension of specie payments by the banks, and the inability of the Administration to carry on the Government, without further legislation by Congress.

This extra session accomplished but little or nothing in the way of public legislation, for the opinion of a majority of Congress was not in unison with that of the President on the questions of Finance and the Independent Treasury. Mr. Williams steadfastly supported the Administration in its financial policy, though from his habits of mind and course of life strongly opposed to any sudden or radical change of measures. At this time a man of wealth, having been many years interested in a bank, and free from all sympathy with the vindictive hatred of banks which characterized so many politicians in Congress, he yet felt that the circumstances of the country justified the plan of an Independent Treasury, dispensing altogether with the aid of banks, providing a set of officers to take charge of the public money, and requiring moreover the payment of all public dues exclusively in specie.

As an original question, few men of high intelligence doubted the wisdom of the measure, but the certainty that it must work an entire revolution in the mode of conducting public business, and largely diminish the value of property, excited the most intense and powerful opposition, and it was only finally carried through in 1840, after the most determined enforcement of party discipline. A political revolution was the consequence. But the country acquiesced in the measure, and the subsequent attempt of Mr. Clay and his friends to change this policy, and return to that of a United States Bank, alienated President Tyler from the Whig party, and led to its subsequent defeat.

Mr. Williams saw the practical results of this measure clearly, and from the start, and advised and supported the Bill of the extra session, and the Bill introduced on the 26th of January, 1838, by the Hon. Silas Wright, of New-York, — between whom and Mr. Williams the utmost cordiality always existed, — and supported the Independent Treasury Act of 1840 which became a law.

Mr. Williams's first act of importance in Congress was the Resolution, submitted by him on the 13th of October, 1837, in reference to the Northeastern Boundary, in the words following : —

3 *

" *Resolved,* That the Secretary of War be directed to submit to the Senate, at as early a day as practicable, a plan for the protection of the northern and eastern frontiers of the United States, designating the points to be permanently occupied by garrisons; the auxiliary stations for reserves, and deposits of munitions and other supplies ; the routes to be established for the purpose of maintaining a safe and prompt intercourse between the several stations, and from these with the depots in the interior ; and finally, the minimum force which, in his opinion, will be required to maintain the peace of the country."

His subsequent labors on this matter, hereafter referred to, were abundant, arduous, and effective, and form no unimportant part of our national history.

At the regular session of the Twenty-fifth Congress, on the 4th of December, 1837, Mr. Williams was placed on the Committee on Naval Affairs, and on that for the District of Columbia. His invaluable labors on the latter committee are still gratefully remembered by the people of Washington.

On the 20th of December, 1837, he called for information as to the survey of the Kennebec River.

But the work of this session for which he is most gratefully remembered, and in many respects the one most deserving of praise in his whole public life, was his effort to provide for the relief of the Insane. On the 29th of December, 1837, he reported a bill, from the Committee on the District of Columbia, for the establishment of an Insane Asylum for the District of Columbia, and for the Army, Navy, and Revenue Service of the United States; and on the 2d of January, 1838, made that brief but able and

clear statement of the claims of this class of unfor-
tunates that satisfied the minds of Senators; and on
the 12th of January, 1838, the bill, appropriating
$75,000 for the purpose of its commencement,
passed the Senate, and finally became a law.

This plan of a Government Hospital, thus initi-
ated, has been carried into execution by one of the
most worthy and accomplished of all the sons that
Maine has sent forth into the field of duty, Dr.
Charles H. Nichols, a native of Vassalboro, in our
State, his father an old friend and client of Mr.
Williams. Nothing could be more gratifying than
to observe the almost filial devotion of Dr. Nichols
to his faithful friend; and Mr. Williams, with equal
gratification, witnessed his success, and saw, in 1861,
the completion of his plans for this great work. The
success of the Government Hospital for the Insane is
admitted to be due to the ability, prudence, fidelity,
and good sense of its accomplished Superintendent,
who has guided all the expenditures, from the purchase of the ground to the erection and completion
of the building, — which is, undoubtedly, more perfect
in its structure, its architectural plan and internal
arrangements, than any similar one in the country.
Its farm, on the eastern shore of the Potomac, two
miles south of the Capitol, contains one hundred and
ninety-five acres, and the building is seven hundred
and twenty feet in length. No intelligent stranger
remains in Washington for a day without visiting
this noble institution.

Equally praiseworthy were Mr. Williams's exer-

tions, in conjunction with Benjamin Brown, Esq., of
Vassalboro, for providing relief for the unfortunate
insane of our own State. He made a donation of
ten thousand dollars toward the foundation of the
Maine Insane Hospital, and ever watched its success
with parental care. In their late Report, the Trustees, under date of December 4th, 1862, say : —

" Since the last meeting of the Trustees, one of the early benefactors and founders of this institution has been called to his rest.
We owe it to the goodness of God that such a man as the Hon.
Reuel Williams has lived and labored amongst us. His name and
many worthy deeds will long be remembered with respect and with
gratitude by multitudes. The fact that the foundations of the hospital
were laid principally through his liberality, is too well known to
need any record here. But it may not be so widely known that
the success and prosperity of the hospital are largely attributable to
his constant care and watchfulness over its interests from the time
of its first establishment to the very close of his useful life. For a
long succession of years Mr. Williams was a leading member of the
Board of Trustees, and was unwearied in his labors for securing
the best means for the comfort and cure of all who came within
these walls. And even after he resigned his seat in the Board, he
did not cease to show his deep interest in the institution, and in what-
soever related to its prosperity. Often have present members of the
Board been favored with his judicious suggestions and wise coun-
sels, that have been of important assistance to them in the respon-
sible trust committed to their hands. While, therefore, we would
bow with reverent submission to the All-wise Disposer of all things,
in the bereavement which has befallen us, we would also, with
gratitude to the same great Being, cherish the memory of our
departed friend and councillor, and strive to imitate his virtues."

The Superintendent, in his Report, uses the following language : —

" It may be well to allude in this connection to the loss the hospital has sustained in the death of one of its founders and largest private benefactors. In the decease of Hon. Reuel Williams, a wide gap has been made in the circle of friends of the insane. Early he beheld the wretched condition of this unfortunate class; his eye pitied, and forth from his beneficence flowed that which laid the foundation-pillars of this noble structure. With a father's care he watched over the interests of the hospital from its beginning, spending days of his valuable time in devising means to promote the comfort and well-being of those who had fallen victims to this worst of human ills, and had come hither for relief. For more than fifteen years he was an active member of the Board of Trustees, performing much of the heavy work which devolved upon the Board, without ever receiving a dollar of compensation for his labor; and when advancing years admonished him that it was time to lay aside the cares of public business, and he resigned the office of Trustee, yet his interest in the institution did not abate. Often his thoughts reverted to it, and his steps were directed hither, where his counsel and advice were freely given to facilitate the best good of the Asylum. And now, though he rests from his labors, though his tongue lies silent in the grave, he yet speaks to us, saying: ' Be kind to the unfortunate and afflicted.' "

On the 2d of February, 1838, Mr. Williams submitted in the Senate the following resolution: —

" *Resolved*, That the President of the United States be, and he hereby is requested to communicate to the Senate, in such manner as he may deem proper, all the correspondence recently received and had between this and the Government of Great Britain, and the State of Maine, on the subject of the Northeastern Boundary, which, in his opinion, may be communicated consistently with the public welfare."

This resolution was considered and agreed to, February 5th, 1838.

He made his great speeches on this question on the 14th of May, 1838, and on the 18th of June, 1838. These speeches, and others on the same subject in 1842, are worthy of republication, as specimens of effective public speaking. The "Bangor Democrat," speaking of the speech of May 14th, says: — "Reuel Williams delivered in the Senate a speech, evincing great research, perfect knowledge of the subject, and remarkable power."

On the 22d of December, 1838, Mr. Williams submitted the following resolution, which was considered and adopted: —

"*Resolved*, That the Secretary of War be requested to communicate to the Senate such information as may be in his possession in reference to the defence of the frontier of Maine, and the number of troops now employed within the State, and the posts at which they are stationed."

He opposed the Treaty of Washington, and in secret session, when its ratification took place, he moved its rejection, and that our Government cause the line to be run and marked, according to the stipulations of the former treaty.

The consummation of this treaty was to him a severe personal and political mortification, and his failure to prevent its ratification was one of the regrets of his life. In reply to an inquiry why he did not defeat it, he said: — "I depended on Judge Preble. He pledged to me his word that he would not give his assent to it. I thought I could depend on Judge Preble, and I left Washington for a short visit to the Virginia Springs, with an invalid daughter, thinking the matter safe, and that the assent of the Maine Commissioners would not be given to it. On my return to Washington, I found the Maine Commissioners, after preparing a statement of reasons for their refusal, had signed their names, *consenting* to the treaty, Preble with the rest, and had left for home. The matter had then got beyond the reach of any power of mine."

Mr. Williams's speech·in secret session, in opposition to its ratification, was only an indignant protest against a foregone conclusion, and he bore in silence the imputation attempted to be cast on him, of a want of frankness in relation to this measure, rather than shield his reputation by a profitless attack and discomfiture of those on whom the real responsibility rested.

But it is a credit to Mr. Williams that he saw in advance what every one now so fully understands and admits, not excepting the geographers and statesmen of England, — the entire absurdity and falsity of the British claim.

Mr. Williams was reëlected to the Senate in 1839, for the term of six years from the 4th of March, 1839, but he retained his seat only six years in all, during the sessions of the Twenty-fifth, Twenty-sixth, and Twenty-seventh Congress, resigning in 1843, on account of the magnitude of his private interests, and his indifference to the honors of public life.

It is the reproach of our system of government, in the estimation of intelligent foreigners, that we have no statesmen in public life, because men pursue politics as a trade, from motives of personal ambition, or as a means of livelihood. It is said that we have no *retiring* age for public men; that, after going

through the routine of Congressional life, men turn
up as candidates for Door-keeper, or appear as lobby-
ists in the pay of contractors, or turn contractors
themselves.

It is pleasant to turn to the example of Mr. Williams, as a reply to this satire. Although so many
years in public life, in such varieties of service, he
never sought office, and never accepted it but in
subordination to a sense of duty; and he laid down
his office or surrendered his trust the instant the
duty assigned him was performed. A public and a
private trust he considered equally sacred. In the
National and State councils, in the several commis-
sions he held, and in the management of the various
public duties confided to him, his time and his best
efforts were as conscientiously and fully devoted, as
when engaged in an important lawsuit for an exact-
ing client.

The character of this brief Memoir, and the length
to which it is already drawn, forbid more extended
comment on Mr. Williams's senatorial career, which
was distinguished throughout by marked ability, and
his accustomed fidelity and independence. Some
acts, however, deserve especial mention as indicating
his superiority to party. He opposed Mr. Calhoun's
amendment to the Enlistment Bill, which first pro-
hibited the enlistment of blacks in the naval service;
and he made a speech in favor of, and voted for, the
Tariff of 1842, the great Whig measure of the
Twenty-seventh Congress, which, but for his vote,
would have been defeated. To Senator Bagby, of

Alabama, who made a coarse and abusive speech, in the style of that time by the extreme Southern men, against the people of New England, Mr. Williams coolly replied, telling the Senator from Alabama that, unfortunately, he knew nothing of the people against whom he addressed his remarks, or he would not be guilty of such an act of injustice.

Although a party man, Mr. Williams never threw a strictly party vote, or, in other words, he voted according to his convictions of duty, and would not surrender his judgment to any party. He did what he thought was right, and voted against his party on all questions whenever, in his opinion, they were in error. He fearlessly opposed the Annexation of Texas, and predicted that it would result in a dissolution of the Union or a protracted civil war, an event he lived to witness.

A good illustration of Mr. Williams's character is shown in his course on the question of legislative instructions. On accepting the Senatorship, he avowed his belief in the binding force of instructions, and declared that in case he could not obey the instructions of the Legislature, he would resign. In 1841 the Maine Legislature, being Whig in politics, passed resolutions referring to Mr. Williams's pledge, and instructing him, in general terms, to vote for Whig measures or resign. Mr. Williams presented these resolutions to the Senate, and in a speech, distinguished for its clearness of statement and logical precision, laid down the true rule as to instructions, and declared his readiness to vote for any specific meas-

4

ure required of him, or resign ; but he failed to find anything in the resolutions sufficiently definite to act upon. This ended the matter of instructions, for no attempt to instruct him on any particular question or measure was afterward made, and his exposition may be fairly regarded as the admitted doctrine on that oft-mooted question of former times.

In retiring from the Senate, Mr. Williams left it with the cordial good-will of all its members. A distinguished contemporary, speaking to us of his Senatorial career, uses the following language : —

"I knew Mr. Williams well whilst he and I were together members of the United States Senate. It was then composed of some of the greatest minds that ever adorned that or any other legislative body. Clay, Webster, and Calhoun were conspicuous in that bright galaxy of talent by which they were surrounded. Mr. Williams held a rank and standing of which his constituents and friends might well be proud. He was a member of some of the most important committees, and discharged his duties with great ability. He investigated a subject thoroughly, and in discussing it was always listened to with profound attention.

"He was decided in his political views, but mild and amiable in presenting them. He commanded the respect of all parties, and no man's opinions had greater weight than his on any question before the Senate, when he was known to have brought to bear upon it his great talent for investigation.

"In his private intercourse he was esteemed and respected by all. His political opinions were always so presented as to produce no acerbity of feeling on the part of political opponents. He was unobtrusive in his manners, conciliating in his general deportment, and never failed to command the good opinion of those with whom his personal or business intercourse brought him into contact."

Those only can have realized the true greatness of Mr. Williams, so quietly and unostentatiously did he move among his fellow-men, who saw him in contact with other great men, at the Bar, or in the Senate of the United States. Here he was the peer of the greatest. One of the last, if not the very last cause he argued in Court, out of his county, was the celebrated case of Veazie *versus* Wadleigh, touching certain water and shore rights at Oldtown, on the Penobscot, before the Supreme Court at Bangor, in the fall of 1834, where, as counsel for Wadleigh and Purinton, he argued their cause with ability and success. He was of counsel for these parties in the subsequent trial before Judge Story, in the Circuit Court of the United States at Wiscasset, with Daniel Webster, Judge Shepley, Jonathan P. Rogers, and the writer of this Memoir. On the other side, Jeremiah Mason, Frederic Allen, and W. P. Fessenden appeared as counsel. The case involved important interests, and excited great attention. More time was occupied in the few days that this case was before the Court, in the consultations of counsel, than in the court-room. In these consultations, the most noticeable fact of all was the extraordinary deference which Mr. Webster paid to Mr. Williams. Although one year older than Mr. Williams, and at that time in the full flush of success and in the zenith of his power as master of eloquence and argument, he deferred to Mr. Williams's opinions or suggestions as to a superior, although, by long and careful investigation and preparation, as fully conversant with all the facts, and the law of the case. This high estimate of Mr. Williams, Mr. Webster always retained, amid all their open conflicts, and their subsequent collisions in public life, growing out of the Northeastern Boundary Dispute and the party contests of the time.

One who knew him long and well says : —

"He had a remarkably clear insight into character. Sometimes he withheld his confidence, where apparently it might safely have been given ; but subsequent events rarely failed to show that what was attributed to prejudice was due only to foresight. Frank, honorable, and upright himself, he scorned indirection and trickery in another ; never idle, and always truthful, he despised a sluggard, and detested a liar. His temperament was remarkably calm and equable. In the ups and downs of a long and busy life, he was rarely elated by gains or depressed by losses. He seemed to view the result of whatever he had deliberately undertaken with a philosophical indifference."

Mr. Williams's superiority in public life was seen in his elevation of purpose and freedom from all inferior or unworthy motives. He never considered the effect of his vote, or of a measure under consideration, upon his party or upon himself. He had no anxiety to shape his policy to suit an existing prejudice, or to satisfy an unreasonable demand. He had no aspirations for a higher place, and no desire to retain his seat in the Senate beyond the time when he felt he had accomplished there what good it was possible for him to achieve. As he entered the Senate at a time when the most fearful and gloomy apprehensions overspread the nation, amid financial embarrassments consequent on unwise tariffs; with commercial credit at its lowest point, and the insane cry against the introduction of foreign capital echoed far and wide by

the leaders of the Democratic party; he knew that
the only mode of sustaining public credit was by the
enactment of a Protective Tariff; and the only method
of giving value to property and diffusing prosperity
among the people was by allowing unfortunate debt-
ors to go free under a General Bankrupt law, while
proper encouragement was given to home industry.
He remained in Congress to vote for these measures,
in opposition to the popular feeling of his party, and
he boldly stood up for what he thought was right,
regardless of the clamor of the shallow politicians of
the hour. He left the Senate after these measures
were consummated, with the consciousness and the
conviction that his duties in that field of labor had
been faithfully and fully performed.

The example of Mr. Williams, at a period when the
possession of a place was used as a mere stepping-
stone to another and a higher one, deserves to be held
up for admiration in contrast with the prevailing tendency of the times. No one, or scarcely one, could
be found in office contented with the discharge of its
duties; and we trace to this cause our political
troubles, the derangements of the currency, the slavery agitation, the repeal of the Missouri Compromise, and its consequent evils culminating in the
present civil war.

It will not be thought out of place to refer, in
this connection, as in striking contrast to Mr. Williams's example, to a contemporary statesman a few
months his senior, who departed this life only a few
hours before Mr. Williams, and who, having passed

through all the gradations of public honors and
offices — Governor of the Empire State, Senator in
Congress, Secretary of State, Minister to the Court of
St. James, Vice-President, and finally President of the
United States, left on record by his will, dated Janu-
ary 18, 1860, this memorable confession : —

" I, Martin Van Buren, of the town of Kinderhook, county of
Columbia, and State of New York, heretofore Governor of the
State, and more recently President of the United States, *but for the
last and happiest year of my life a farmer* in my native town, do make
and declare the following to be my last will and testament," &c.

The fact of Van Buren's election to the Presidency
gave him no real satisfaction, for his joy was turned
to sadness, and his cup of happiness poisoned by subsequent defeats; and never did he find so much satisfaction as in the quiet of rural pursuits.   If we recall
the history of other of Mr. Williams's contemporaries
in the Senate, — Clay, Webster, Calhoun, Cass, and
Benton, leaders in those days who never reached the
Presidency ; or Pierce and Buchanan who did, — we
shall be struck with the singular infelicity of their
political career, from disappointments like those of
Van Buren, or worse results than defeat.

We esteem it fortunate that an example like that
of Mr. Williams remains to us, that no feeling of unsatisfied political ambition disquieted his subsequent
life, and that he had the good sense and self-respect
to decline a seat in the Cabinet, virtually proffered
him, for which, by his great experience on the Committee on Naval Affairs in the Senate and his admirable executive ability, he was so preëminently

qualified. But greater than all was the value of his example, in the healthfulness of its tone, in his freedom from those "infirmities of genius" that regard imprudence in personal habits, extravagance, and debauchery as the necessary conditions of public life. It was the fault of the time to regard politicians as necessarily heedless and improvident, and that for them there must be pensions and subscriptions, as if such men were not expected to foresee the consequences of their own weakness and folly. Mr. Williams saw all this in its true light, — that the only true basis of political power and influence was a lofty independence that scorned alike the thought that a pension was a mark of honor, or that his party had any right to treat him as a hireling and a mendicant. Simple in his habits, generous in his mode of living, he made no concessions of his personal independence to any of the arbitrary and capricious demands of fashion or of party, and pursued the even tenor of his way, not only in the Senate, but in all his private walks to the close of his earthly career. His whole life in business, in the family circle, and in public station, seemed, in a measure, mechanical, — like a well-ordered machine, where each part, obeying its organic law, in subordination to a higher principle, ran on, with an unvarying and steady movement, till it fulfilled its mission, and the fine frame that held the informing spirit ceased to move.

At the ripe age of sixty, in the full strength of his intellectual and physical powers, without any unsatisfied desire, he resigned his seat in the Senate, with

two years more of his term before him, in the full
expectation of retiring altogether from public service.
But new labors awaited him. The country rapidly
recovered from its six years of exhaustion — from
1836 to 1842 — under the influence of the Tariff of
1842, and in 1844 the spirit of improvement reached
Maine, and her people began to entertain the subject
of railroads. The drain on its population consequent
on the building of railways and factories in Massachusetts and elsewhere, with the tendency to emigrate
West, had begun to draw upon the strength of the
State, and to excite alarm ; and it was seen and felt
that, in spite of the limited amount of our realized
capital, Maine must embark in these improvements
or fall behind in the race.

Mr. Williams looked upon these movements as premature ; and in the winter of 1843-4, when the project of a railway from Portland to Bath was acted on,
he took very little if any interest in it. In the
western portion of the State, an intense and bitter
hostility to railways had been engendered, by the
course adopted in the construction of a line into
Portland by parties residing out of the State, in extension of the line from Boston. This feeling had
full sway in the Legislature of 1844, and no satisfactory charter could be obtained. Legislation of the
most hostile character against existing lines of railway was carried through, in sympathy with the feeling in New Hampshire. The railway question had
been made a political party question, the Whigs
favoring, and the Democratic party opposing. Mr.

Williams had no sympathy with this party feeling, but he knew the expensive character of railways, and saw no means adequate to their immediate construction, and that their first effect would be to carry off business from the State.

In the autumn of 1844, when the plan of a railway from Montreal to the Atlantic was proposed, the design was to have two outlets—one to reach the ocean at Portland, and the other, embranching in the Androscoggin Valley at Rumford or Bethel, to extend to Augusta, and from thence to Bangor eastward, and to Bath.

The people of Portland promptly fell into the support of the project; those of Augusta disregarded the proposal. The Montreal Railway project took immediate possession of the public mind of the State. The "Eastern Argus," the leading organ of the Democratic party, took the strongest ground in its support, and its conductors made no secret of their design to throw party overboard on the railway question, and, if need be, break down their party in the State on it, rather than longer forego the advantages of railroads.

The result was not long doubtful. The leaders of both parties vied with each other in their zeal for railways; and by a single stride, with scarcely any opposition, Maine changed front on the railway question, and adopted the most liberal policy of any State in the Union. This unanimity of sentiment was Maine's chief capital; and thinking men foresaw the result, in the sure accomplishment of the great-

est public work of the day, taking into account
its international character, and its influence on the
course of trade and of public opinion. The geo-
graphical and commercial importance of Maine was
in a measure realized by the more intelligent of its
people.

The putting of this project into execution led to
the adoption of another — the extension of a line in
connection with the Montreal Railroad to Bangor
and the East. The development of this plan roused
the lower Kennebec, and her people came forward
with a renewal of their project — a line of railway from Portland to Augusta, with a branch to
Bath.

These rival movements aroused the whole State,
including Mr. Williams, who, from his great wealth,
known sagacity, and public spirit, was necessarily to
become a leader in them. Yet he held back rather
than pressed forward at the start. But events
moved rapidly. An effort to unite all interests in
the State, by swinging the Trunk Line to Montreal
as far east as Lewiston, an extension thence to Gar-
diner and up the Kennebec River, with a branch to
Brunswick and Bath, failed of success, from the unwillingness of Mr. Williams and his associates to desert the line of policy unfortunately agreed on with
the leading citizens of Bath and Brunswick.

Two rival schemes went forward, soon involving a
war of the gauges, for the Atlantic and St. Lawrence
Railroad Company and the Androscoggin and Kennebec Railroad Company adopted an independent

guage of five and a half feet, upon the fullest consideration of its advantages, while the Kennebec and Portland Railroad Company adhered to the plan of a narrow-gauge line, in view of a connection with the line of railway to Boston.

From the autumn of 1846, the war of rival interests was fiercely waged, subordinating nearly all, if not every other public question in the State to this, till, on the completion of the "*Back Route*" to Waterville, in advance of the construction of the narrow-gauge line to Augusta, Mr. Williams frankly admitted their great error. He entered the Legislature in 1848, as the Representative from Augusta, and endeavored to break the chain of charters that held in check all extension of railways above Augusta, in connection with the narrow gauge, but in this he was for the time defeated. He had not over-estimated his own power, so much as he had undervalued the strength of his opponents. He saw clearly the disastrous consequences to his own fortune of the policy of rival lines, and he frankly inquired for conditions of peace. Those agreed on were, an abandonment of any purpose to extend a rival line on the narrow gauge to Bangor, and the unanimous support of a broad-gauge line from Waterville east, with suitable arrangements for connection at the point of crossing of the narrow-gauge line from Augusta up the Kennebec River.

This arrangement, on his part, was faithfully observed and kept; the restriction on the right to extend a line from Augusta up the Kennebec River was taken off, and the broad-gauge line was extended from Waterville, in connection with the Androscoggin and Kennebec Railroad, to Bangor.

Mr. Williams took great interest in the project of the railway from Bangor to St. John and Halifax, attended the celebration at the breaking of ground on the European and North-American Railway, at St. John, was a director in the Maine corporation, and a party to the provisional contract for the construction of the line through Maine, by Jackson and Betts, which fell through from a failure to secure the necessary legislation in Maine, on account of the opposition of parties interested in the contract for building the line from Waterville to Bangor. The Crimean War soon after followed, and the people of Bangor discovered, when it was too late, their error in not allowing the granting of a charter, adequate to the requirements of the enterprise. But for this short-sightedness, the entire capital for the line from Waterville to Halifax would have been provided, before the European war of 1853–4 had disturbed the money market of England.

This railway war, in our State, has been the prolific cause of disaster to many a private fortune, and embittered, for the time, some sections against others. But such is the peculiar configuration of the State, and so great was the isolation from each other of the various sections before the advent of railways, that, from want of unity in purpose and plan, it may fairly be doubted if a single line could so soon have gone forward and been extended to

Bangor, or to the Kennebec, but for this rivalry. The public, as a whole, were the gainers, but there was a painful loss entailed on the original stockholders and bondholders. Of this class Mr. Williams was the largest loser. He invested of his own fortune more than three hundred thousand dollars, and sacrificed more than two thirds of that sum in this railroad, to say nothing of the indirect losses that followed, and the devotion of more than fifteen years of his life. But when the sacrifice had been made, he looked philosophically at the result, and said : " I do not, on the whole, regret it. I doubt if my time and money could have accomplished so much good in any other way." Some things had stung him deeply; such as the repudiation of original liability, pleaded by way of defence, on a suit on coupons, upon certain city bonds which had been issued to aid the construction of the Kennebec and Portland Railroad, of which he was the President; as if the plea of payment was not sufficient, or all that an honorable defence would justify. He also felt the injustice of the refusal, by his associates, of that support which they had promised him in the hour of the greatest pecuniary difficulties of the Railroad Company, in case he gave out his own personal obligations, to avoid the sacrifice impending over it. But he was too much a man of the world to make private griefs public, and suffered in silence the consequences of his own generosity and public spirit.

It is true Mr. Williams had, of necessity, kept a

5

show of courage amid the difficulties that surrounded the construction of so expensive a line of railroad, or its ruin would have been inevitable. But he refused to desert his post, or take any advantage to himself. He relied upon that good faith and that sense of honor which he himself respected, and saw, in his old age, the dropping out, one after another, of those on whose good faith he had relied for agreed contributions toward his advances, with the same sort of feeling as one looks at the follies of youth, "more in sorrow than in anger." Wearied with the delays of the Court in deciding controverted points, he made the best terms he could by amicable adjustment of his claims, and philosophically gave his thoughts to other matters. Other men contributed liberally, some perhaps as freely as himself, in proportion to their means, but it is not hazarding anything to say that, but for Mr. Williams, the railroad could not so soon, if ever, have been built to Augusta.

No man in our State, or in New England, ever passed through such a trial of strength, both of character and fortune, as Mr. Williams suffered for fifteen years, from the time of the inception of the railroad enterprise till he closed his connection with it in 1861. His hitherto unconquered will regarded no labor too arduous, no effort of mind too great, no sacrifice of private fortune too large, for the successful accomplishment of what he deemed a necessary public work; while he, at the same time, realized what all men of true public spirit and of generous natures know, that, for any great work done for the public, the only present reward will be the ill-will of the sluggish, the envy of the narrow-minded, and the hatred of all those most benefited by his labors.

But death robs envy of its sting, and a wiser appreciation of the value to themselves of the labor of another gradually eradicates the hatred of compeers and competitors. De Witt Clinton was deprived of his office as Canal Commissioner, the emoluments of which were esteemed by him as a means of support of a large family, as he declined to profit from public employment; but a returning sense of justice has made his name renowned and honored everywhere.

Having closed an agreement for the sale of his interest in the railroad, in September, 1861, Mr. Williams again became free of public cares. But new duties still awaited him. In the month of October following, though then in the seventy-eighth year of his age, he yielded to the earnest solicitation of Governor Washburn, and accepted the appointment of Commissioner of Maine to Washington, in response to the invitation of the United States Government, to inaugurate a system of defences for the loyal States. This Commission was dated the 23d of October, 1861, and on the 1st of November Mr. Williams reached Washington in the discharge of its duties, — his first visit since his resignation of the office of Senator eighteen years before. One only of the old *employés* of the Senate of his time remained. Asbury Dickens, Secretary of the Senate, had, a few months before, at the age of ninety-four, been gathered to his fathers,

and the Senate Chamber of 1843 had been assigned
to the Supreme Court, and new Halls, with ample
apartments, were now occupied by the Senate and
the House.   Elisha Whittlesey, the upright First
Comptroller of the Treasury, of the same age with
himself, was discharging with his accustomed vigor
the duties of his office.   But he, too, has recently been
called away at the summons of death.   A few men of
other days remained of those in office when Mr. Williams left public life.   But it was a pleasing sight to
witness the deference everywhere paid him, for no
man ever left Washington with a purer reputation.

Mr. Williams grew impatient at times at the delays
consequent on the absence of the public officials, but
remained some weeks, until an agreement was made
with the Administration that it would enter at once
upon the defence of the State, and accept the money
needed therefor from the State Treasury, on the issue
to it, in return, of twenty years six per cent. bonds.

On the receipt of the official note of the Secretary
of War, setting forth the terms of the arrangement,
Mr. Williams left for Maine.   But before his departure
he joined in an application to the Secretary of War
for the putting in progress the work on the Fort at
the mouth of the Kennebec, and another for giving
it the name it now bears, both of which were successful.

This was the close of his public life.   Up to this
time, no one could perceive any diminution of his
powers of mind, and scarcely any abatement of his
physical activity, except a slight defect in hearing

and a more measured gait. At Washington he visited all the public places and military parades, regardless of the weather; climbed all the staircases and galleries of the new Capitol, the Insane Hospital, and the various public offices, with apparent ease; and he received and returned calls from his numerous friends of other days.

He had urged, as an objection to his acceptance of this Commission from Governor Washburn, the fact of his age, and his unwillingness to take a place calling for active service that could be better performed by another and younger man. But on learning fully Governor Washburn's policy, and perceiving how deeply he felt the necessity of his acceptance of that trust, he yielded his objections; for he realized the importance of the occasion, and the value of the opportunity afforded by this invitation of the President for establishing the claims of Maine upon the General Government, and of initiating a policy for the State.

It proved what Governor Washburn intimated to him might possibly turn out to be the case, — "his last public service, the graceful rounding off of a long life of public usefulness and duty." The complete success of the Commission, and the unanimity with which the Legislature of Maine adopted and followed out the policy of Governor Washburn, was to Mr. Williams a grateful and satisfactory reward. He regarded the policy thus entered upon as destined to final and full success, requiring only the persistent efforts of the State Government to this end.

5 *

Returning from Washington in November, 1861, he was taken down with a severe attack of catarrhal fever, probably aggravated, if not induced, by the excitements and exposures of his long journey. For some time his recovery seemed doubtful. But his iron frame withstood the attack, and after some months of confinement he regained sufficient strength to attend to business, — a new call being made upon him to rebuild, on the site of his former office, an elegant and more valuable block of stores, in place of one swept away by fire. He went into this work with his accustomed energy. He carried out, too, in June, 1862, his purpose of a business visit to Boston. On his return from Boston, on the 4th of July, his friends were, for the first time, admonished of his failing strength. He soon perceived this himself, and said: — "I do not get any stronger; and I do not know as I desire to." But a day before his death, though confined to his house, he seemed so well that his son went to Portland on business, not deeming him so near his end.

On the 24th of July he sank rapidly, and was fully conscious of the approach of death. Observing his only brother near him, he quietly said, " You have come to see the last of me, Daniel; we may as well take leave of each other now," and they shook hands.

To his granddaughter, who was in the room at eleven o'clock in the evening, and of whom he was very fond, he said, " You had better go to bed, Anna," and he kissed her and sent her away.

Calm and unruffled, as in the days of his manly strength, he cheerfully awaited the summons of death with the dignity of a philosopher and the meekness of a Christian. At one o'clock on the morning of Friday, July 25th, 1862, the life of Reuel Williams on earth was no more.

In this hurried and imperfect sketch of the more salient features of Mr. Williams's career, doubtless many things are omitted which might have been appropriately referred to, had the duty fallen on the writer of it in season for a fuller preparation, or at a time when his thoughts could have been uninterruptedly given to it. A sense of obligation to the illustrious deceased, and a vivid appreciation of the eminence of his virtues and the greatness of his character, alone justified this effort to place in the archives of our Society some facts calculated to perpetuate his memory. The task should have fallen on one nearer his own age, more familiar with his early life, and better fitted by habits of study, and as a writer, to do justice to so noble a man.

Numerous, varied, and invaluable as were Mr. Williams's public labors, they were far less deserving of praise than his private life. Public employment sometimes destroys or unfits one for the duties of a good citizen, often the most trying of all. Mr. Williams's public and professional labors did not withdraw his attention from the ordinary duties of daily life as a citizen, a neighbor, and a friend. The care of schools, the education of the young, the opening

of highways, the establishment of lines of communication by means of stage-coaches and of steamboats,
before the advent of railways, were among the matters carefully looked after by him, as well as the
building of churches, hotels, and other public edi-
fices.   He was an advocate, and an exemplar, too, of
the doctrine of "encouragement to home industry,"
in the building of foundries, factories, and other
works for employing labor and capital.   He was the
chief promoter, if not the original projector, of that
noble line of stages between Augusta and Bangor,
which had no superior in the United States.   He had
a large interest in the Augusta Dam, built in 1837.
Though slow to come into the plan of building it,—
distrustful, inasmuch as it had, at its inception, no
secure ledge foundation,—after it was once entered upon, he gave to it his generous support, and
finally the whole rested on his shoulders.   When this
dam was carried away in 1839, creating so much
consternation and alarm, he alone of all the people
of the city, was calm and unruffled.   An eminent
lawyer of his own age, speaking of him, says : " His
firmness and immovability were strongly tested in
disaster as well as in success ; the reminiscent saw
him, immediately after the destruction of the Kennebec Dam at Augusta ; when every one else seemed
excited and agitated, he alone was calm and tran-
quil."

Subsequently, when the ledge revealed itself on
the western shore of the river, Mr. Williams's confidence in the dam was established.   Valuable invest-

ments in the shape of factories and workshops are now planted there, in which he was largely interested.

It has been shown by a recent writer that great vital power is essential to eminent success; that no man has reached the highest attainments in science, art, law, politics, or arms, without extraordinary vital force. Without this organic power, no one can sustain that intense, long-continued application, that is essential to the mastery of the more difficult problems in abstract science, or the practical solution of the novel questions that arise in public affairs.

Mr. Williams, no doubt, owed much of his success to his naturally fine, physical organization. Not large, or much above the average of men in physical stature, he had a close-knit, compact, sturdy, muscular frame. The labors of early life strengthened his bodily powers, which his cheerful temper, upright life, and industrious habits, kept free of all excesses, so that he never wasted his life physically, nor his mind by any indolence or neglect, while his moral sense had all the instinctive quickness of a sensitive nature, rendered active by watchful practice; so that he had in early life the most extraordinary self-reliance and self-control, and he seemed to those who knew him far older than his years, and almost too precise and methodical for a man of ordinary impulses.

A striking trait in Mr. Williams's character was a habit of early rising, commenced in boyhood, and continued through life. He was always prompt at

his post, whether at school, in his office, or other position.   He invariably took the earliest hours of the
morning for the performance of labor, and was thus
enabled to accomplish more than others.   By systematic use of time, he achieved more, in the fruits
of labor, than any one known to me.   He could sustain the most exhausting intellectual effort without
apparent fatigue.   He had extraordinary powers of
abstraction, so that he could give his mind fully to
the investigation of any required subject, withdraw-
ing his thoughts from other topics, till he mastered
all its details of fact and comprehended the principles involved ; and then turn his mind upon another
matter equally difficult, without any confusion of
ideas or loss of perceptive power.   When his mind
had been called to examine a question, he held on to
it till he saw all its bearings and relations clearly
and distinctly, and his mind never wavered or hesi-
tated as to its conclusions.   These traits were early
developed, and by this means he could readily dis-
pose of a vast number of difficult questions, which
ordinarily would embarrass and perplex men of less
clearness of perception and less strength of purpose.

But his great peculiarity was a habit of system
and order.   He did one thing at a time, and finished
it before he allowed his mind to be distracted by
other matters.   It was this habit, readily acquired
and formed in early life, that enabled him to accomplish so much, with such uniform success.   He was
an accurate copyist in boyhood, a sagacious business
man on his entrance into the legal profession, a wise

counsellor in the more difficult cases that arise in practice, an apt conveyancer and draughtsman, — remarkable for the terse brevity of his legal instruments, — a skilful pleader in the days of technical practice, and an effective and successful advocate. To the jury and before the court his arguments were able, logical, and exhaustive.

This habit of doing a thing thoroughly and at the first, and so arranging all his books and papers as to lose no time in a confused search for what he wanted, made him the remarkable business man that he continued to be through life. He never allowed himself to add a column of figures a second time, and never found himself, or was found by others, to be mistaken.

To all who knew him well Mr. Williams's domestic life was the most charming theatre of his virtues; for amid all the activity of business, and the calls on his time in the public service, he never neglected his own fireside, or forgot his parental duties. Not his own children and household alone, but the large family circle of which he became the recognized and honored head, felt his influence, and the power of his teachings. His own self-denying example, his even temper, his affable manners, his fidelity to duty in all the minute details of daily life, his readiness to aid those who were disposed to help themselves, and his silent but stern rebuke of all levity and extravagance, exerted a powerful effect on all, especially on the young, who came within the reach of his influence. His brothers and sisters, his nephews and nieces alike, consulted him and leaned on his advice with affectionate veneration and regard. He threw himself into the sports of children with the same zest as into business, always excelling in any of them. He was very fond of children and young persons, and yearly or oftener, as occasion favored, even in his latest years, he would get an omnibus, and, filling it with children, grandchildren, and friends, go off to Togus, or elsewhere, on a strawberry party, or on some expedition of pleasure. He was also very fond of fishing, and, when practicable, would give up his birthday, with a week's time, to this sport.

Notwithstanding his naturally reserved manner and demeanor to strangers, or those whose character he did not respect, he was as mild and gentle as a child in disposition, and most cordial and winning to those who appreciated his true character.

His professional life, as such, gave him no great opportunity for wide notoriety or distinction out of his State, and probably he had less pride in his profession merely as a profession, than most men of his time of far less ability. His great success in the early acquisition of an ample fortune through his own un-aided exertions, his large acquaintance with the leading men of Massachusetts of that day, his annual visits of some weeks to Boston, where he met in the familiarity of friendship the best educated and most accomplished gentlemen of that city, seemed to satisfy his ambition, without effort for public notoriety. But he was widely known, in comparatively early life, as a man of high promise; while his entire self-possession, ease of manner, and self-reliance, early led to his recognition as a perfect gentleman, though he never *assumed* to be one.   His accurate knowledge, clear judgment, unquestioned integrity, admirable business qualities, and well-known success, inspired general confidence at home and abroad, and gave him vast influence over the people of the community where he dwelt ; and his singular freedom from all vanity, display, or affectation of superiority, disarmed the natural jealousy evinced toward prominent men ; and he was popular beyond example, for one possessing his positive qualities.   It may be doubted if any man can be named who had in so great a degree, for so long a lifetime, retained so fully the unqualified confidence of the entire community in which he lived.   He enjoyed, too, in an equal degree, the confidence and good-will of his brethren of the legal profession, — the highest aim and end of a lawyer's life.

Everything that Mr. Williams said or did, in public or private, was the result of conviction.   He was sincere in thought and in act.   He did nothing for effect, nothing to excite attention, or draw forth observation and remark.   His desire was to do his duty, to fulfil with scrupulous exactness every obligation, whether arising from his own act or undertaking, or resulting from that of others, in all the varied relations of life, whether in the family circle, the neighborhood, the community, or the world at large.   He had an abiding faith in his own judgment, for he sought to form it by the pursuit and observance of every honorable method to gain information, with the

6

most conscientious desire to reach the exact measure of justice to others.

It may be proper to say something as to his religious belief. Educated in the Congregational order of early days, before its division into Orthodox and Unitarian sects, he afterwards became a member of the latter, and was a liberal supporter of that denomination. In May, 1853, in the Unitarian Church, occupied for the time by the Rev. Robert C. Waterston, of Boston, Mr. Williams was publicly baptized. This event following soon after the death of his son-in-law, the Rev. Mr. Judd, a man of rare genius and of deep religious feeling, for many years pastor of that church, shows the influence that had gradually led him to make a public confession of his faith.

To extraordinary energy, Mr. Williams united a large share of common sense. He had a well-balanced mind, with excellent judgment, without any brilliant qualities of any sort. These gave him great success. His influence with the jury was most remarkable, from the confidence felt in his sincerity and the truth of his statements. He had the power of presenting such arguments and reasonings as would satisfy the common sense and ordinary understandings of men. His sense of justice was always predominant. In testifying to facts affecting his own interests, no one could fail to see his exact regard for truth, and his anxious desire to give full force to facts adverse to his own side of the case. Instances of this sort are abundant and familiar to our courts and lawyers.

He had no sympathy with persons infirm of purpose, or deficient in energy and courage. He felt that success in this world was open to all men alike, and he had no patience with a spendthrift or a sluggard, though ready to help the unfortunate and the deserving.

A form of beneficence practised by Mr. Williams, most valued and most valuable, was the encouragement he gave to the industrious and deserving, who had been fortunate enough to gain his good-will, giving them means of acquiring independence by the judicious loan of his capital, in the form of permanent rents at low rates, or advances made in view of contemplated success in business. The proprieties of private confidence forbid more than an allusion to this noble trait of Mr. Williams's character.

Trained in the severest discipline in the daily duties of early life, instinctively fond of order and method, he enjoyed to the last the labors of business, the watchfulness of parental oversight, and the care of his own property. In private, as in public life, he was faithful and faultless; as a legislator, cautious and conservative. He had an instinctive regard for the common law, and dreaded the innovations of sentimental theorists. All changes of the law of descent, and the separation of the property of husband and wife, he spoke of with disfavor, as tending to disturb domestic tranquillity; and he regarded the sacredness of pecuniary obligation as essential to the maintenance of good morals.

But he never took advantage of the misfortunes, the weaknesses, or the mistakes of others. He never exacted a harsh penalty, or claimed a forfeiture, against an unfortunate or imprudent debtor, or took unlawful interest of others. His fortune was largely due to sagacious investments in lands, at an early day, but more to his systematic industry, and the gradual accumulations of a long life of patient and productive toil.

Though occupied by so many and such multiform cares of private and public business, he had abundant leisure for the gratification of every wish, for he so arranged his business matters that they never encroached upon one another.

Many acts of charity on the part of Mr. Williams were so performed as to leave no feeling of mortification in the recipients of his generosity; and he was ever careful to avoid all acts that might in any way needlessly wound the pride of those less fortunate than himself in the acquisition of wealth. His sense of justice was the mainspring of his conduct, and he followed the dictates of his judgment far more than any impulses of feeling.

If we were called upon to determine in what aspect of his life his example was of most value, we should say in the practical solution of that greatest social problem of this age, — the proper uses of wealth, — a question especially interesting to Americans, from the comparative ease with which it is obtained, and the laxity of morals which seems naturally to follow its possession. For distinguished position or great wealth, unaccompanied by that refinement and culture which insure their direction to noble ends, is a positive evil to the possessor, as well as to society at large; and the man who has wealth without generosity and public virtue, is an incumbrance if not a nuisance in society. To treat with respect the opinions or the memory of a man who has money, for that alone, but who fails to fulfil the arduous and self-denying trusts which wealth always and necessarily imposes, indicates a debasement in morals as offensive as the worship of idols, or other practices that place savage below civilized life. In any proper estimate of a man's character, we must award praise or blame by that impartial estimate that future times will recognize as the true one — the amount of good or ill he has accomplished for humanity and his race. Any standard of virtue drawn from a more limited view of its nature than its adaptation to the general laws of our well-being, would be unworthy of our assent; and we estimate a man's greatness in proportion to the conformity of his life to these principles.

Upon any view of life, therefore, judging by the lowest standard of virtue, few men are fortunate within the definition of the uninspired Greek moralist, and still smaller the number of those worthy of remembrance after death. Domestic infelicity, infirmity of body, a lack of the means of enjoyment in early life of the aspirations of youthful ambition, the want of opportunity to fall bravely in battle for one's country, or by some honorable sacrifice win an honored name in death, are the common allotments of humanity. It is only those whose life has developed the persistent, self-denying principles of virtue, that future ages can worthily honor.

As Mr. Williams recedes from the immediate view of his contemporaries, his character will loom up to the eye of those who come after us, and assume its true proportions among his compeers. Men of more brilliant talent — in the popular language of the day — or even more developed in a single quality of mind, were around him, in the Senate and in our own State. Others had more attainments in knowledge derived from books, others still had more powers of oratorical fascination, than he ever put forth in action. But it is in vain to seek among them all for one who united, in so eminent a degree, all the true elements of manhood with so few defects; who illustrated the self-denying virtue of patient forbearance under trials the most perplexing, of fidelity to duty under the greatest temptation to self-aggrandizement, of generous magnanimity under the most mortifying proofs of ingratitude. With every opportunity for self-indulgence, he maintained to the last the virtues of an almost austere simplicity with the wisest private and public generosity, realizing the measure of Solon's rule, that he to whom Divinity continued happiness unto the end we call happy.